Pup
Patrol

Farm
Rescue

DARREL and
SALLY ODGERS

Illustrated by
JANINE DAWSON

Kane Miller
A DIVISION OF EDC PUBLISHING

In loving memory of Darrel's dad, Roy Odgers,
and Sally's mum, Pat Farrell.
- Darrel and Sally Odgers

For Lyn & Gill
- Janine Dawson

First American Edition 2016
Kane Miller, A Division of EDC Publishing

Text copyright © Sally and Darrel Odgers 2015
Internal illustrations copyright © Janine Dawson 2015

First published by Scholastic Press a division of Scholastic Australia Pty Limited in 2015.
Cover illustration by Heath McKenzie.

For information contact:
Kane Miller, A Division of EDC Publishing
PO Box 470663
Tulsa, OK 74147-0663
www.kanemiller.com
www.edcpub.com
www.usbornebooksandmore.com

Library of Congress Control Number: 2015954250

Printed and bound in the United States of America

6 7 8 9 10

ISBN: 978-1-61067-518-5

Dear Readers,

My name is **Barnaby Station Stamp of Approval,** but you can call me Stamp. My friend Ace and I travel around the country with James Barnaby in a vehicle we call **the Fourby.** I am a **border collie,** so you won't be surprised to learn that I am handsome and clever. Ace is clever too, but James says her second name is Trouble. Ace is not a border collie. She is a mongrel, a dog of mixed breed.

The story you are about to read is our first big Pup Patrol adventure. James and I had been traveling for just three weeks. We hadn't met Ace yet. But don't worry, she comes later. Everything was wonderful, until it started to rain . . .

Yours,

Stamp

Pup Patroller

Stamp's Glossary

Barnaby Station Stamp of Approval.
Pedigreed animals often have long names.
My parents are named Barnaby Station Penny
Black and Brightwood Superlative.

Border collies. Herding dogs that came from
the Anglo-Scottish borders. They are one of the
most intelligent dogs in the world.

The Fourby. Four-wheel drive SUV.

Chapter One

Rain

"Baaaa! Baaaaaa! *Baaaaaddddd!*" Sheep in a panic make a **pawful** lot of noise.

"Can we take the boat to rescue them?" James shouted. (He had to shout over the noise of the rain, the sheep and the river.) "Stamp and your dog work well together. They can help by keeping the sheep in a bunch."

"Too risky," yelled Glen Pepper. Rain dripped off his long nose. "Look at that!"

He pointed as a whole tree tore past us on the flood. "If that hit the boat, we'd tip over!"

Rusty, the old border collie, barked once, sharply. Then he growled, "Do something! Quickly!" to Glen.

Glen stared at the sheep and shook his head. Rain poured down. It was like having a big bucket of water tipped over us.

"Why are humans so slow?" said Rusty. "Those sheep need help!"

"Wait a bit," I said. "Let's—"

I never finished what I was about to say. One minute Rusty stood right there beside me, his ears and eyebrows streaming with water. The next . . . he leapt out into the river and disappeared.

So, why were James and I standing in the rain with a long-nosed man and an old dog, staring at stranded sheep?

It started one afternoon as we drove the Fourby along the coast, on our way to Cowfork. We'd been having a wonderful time, camping along the way. James and I both love to run so we often stopped in interesting places and raced one another up hills and down twisty-turny tracks. If we met other people and dogs, we'd stop to have what Dad Barnaby calls **"a yarn."**

Things were **pawfect** until the weather changed. By now, drizzle had been falling for three days. The floor of the Fourby was muddy. The windows were fogging up. James's hair was damp. The Fourby smelled of **wet dog**. That was me, of course.

James and I were fed up. We wished we were back at **Barnaby Station**.

"It's going to be another cold night, Stamp," said James. "The tent's still wet from last night."

I gave a small whine of agreement. Like most border collies, I understand a lot of human words, although of-paws I can't *say* them. I thumped my tail. I knew we'd work something out. We always do. I leaned against James's shoulder, wetting his shirt.

"That settles it," said James, nudging me off. "We're going to find a dry place to sleep tonight."

The drizzle chose that moment to turn into heavy rain. James switched the windshield wipers up as high as they would go. Rivers of water swished off and ran down the windows.

After a bit, James pulled the Fourby over to the side of the road and unfolded the map. "Okay," he said. "We're several hours from Cowfork, but quite close to

Glen and Wendy Pepper's place at Pepper Plains. What do you think, Stamp?"

I pawed at the map.

"Pepper Plains it is," said James.

We set off again. As James drove along, I looked out the window. Even over the Fourby's engine and the rain on the roof, I could hear a roaring sound. A train? I pricked up my ears.

"I guess that's the Jeandabah River," said James. "It sounds a lot bigger than it looks on the map. Ah, here we are. There's the sign for Pepper Plains." He turned the vehicle onto a gravel road. Well, it was probably gravel, but at the moment it was more like mud.

It was still pouring when we reached the homestead at Pepper Plains Farm. James parked the Fourby and we dashed for the doorstep.

I got there first. James runs fast, but I run faster. By the time James caught up, I had shaken the rain off my fur and was sitting on the doorstep.

"Show-off," said James. He tapped the door knocker.

The woman who answered the door was about as old as Mum Barnaby. She

smelled of vegetable soup. She looked a bit surprised to see a wet young man and a wet (but handsome) border collie on her doorstep.

James smiled. "Hello, Mrs. Pepper. Remember me?"

The woman stared at us for a moment. "James Barnaby! What in the world are you doing here? Are your parents with you?"

"No, it's just us, Mrs. P. We're on a bit of a camping trip," said James.

"In *this* weather?" said Mrs. Pepper. "Why do people insist on camping in the rain?"

"It wasn't raining when we left home," said James.

A few minutes later, we were sitting in front of the fire. James's shirt and my coat steamed gently. The whole room smelled of vegetable soup and wet dog.

Mrs. Pepper gave James a towel. "That's a handsome dog," she said, as James started to rub me dry.

I gave Mrs. Pepper **a stamp of approval**.

"This is Stamp," said James. "I chose him from Penny Black's last litter. Dad says I picked myself a champion."

"When he's dry, you can shut him in the barn," said Mrs. Pepper.

The barn? Maybe she didn't deserve my stamp of approval.

Stamp's Glossary

Barnaby Station. This is a big farm where I was born and where my mother, Penny Black, still lives. James's parents, Mum and Dad Barnaby, live there too.

Champion. A champion dog is one who is clever, well behaved, skilled, handsome and likely to win lots of prizes. Just like me.

Having a yarn. Talking and getting to know someone. Friendly humans do it.

Pawfect. Perfect, for dogs.

Pawful. Awful, for dogs.

The smell of wet dog. Has nothing to do with being dirty. It's all about being a dog and being wet.

Stamp of approval. An award for being clever, kind and all-around fine. Only I can give this award.

Chapter Two

In The Barn

"Thanks, Mrs. P.," said James. "The barn will be a lot drier than our tent."

I looked up at him and grumbled.

Glen Pepper came in then. "I thought you'd be at college this year," he said to James after they had **shaken hands**.

"I'm taking a year off to see the country," said James. "It was great until the weather changed."

"There's more rain on the way,

according to the forecast," said Glen. "You'd better stay here for a while."

"Thanks," said James. "Stamp and I will work for you until it clears up." He grinned. "Dad says a man and his dog can do a lot to help out if they turn up at the right place at the right time."

James fetched our things from the Fourby. I was happy to see he had remembered my favorite **wool blanket**. He hung it near the fire to air and gave me a bowl of kibble. I backed behind the couch while the humans ate dinner. If I stayed out of sight Mrs. Pepper might forget about shutting me in the barn.

Mrs. Pepper did not forget.

"Best go and tie your dog up in the barn now," she said after dinner, "while I make you up a bed here."

"Thank you, but I'll sleep in the barn

with Stamp," said James.

"That's just silly," said Mrs. Pepper.

"I really would like to sleep in the barn," said James gently.

"But—"

"Thanks for dinner, Mrs. P." James smiled at her. "Is there anything I can do to help first?"

Glen Pepper sighed. "Not unless you know how to turn off the rain."

Mrs. Pepper fetched a couple of blankets and a pillow for James. "I'm sure your sleeping bag is damp," she said. "Put it on the drying rack for the night with any damp clothes."

James did that and then we took our lantern, my blanket and James's bedding and dashed across to the barn.

We made ourselves comfortable in the hay and James went to sleep. (Mum

Barnaby says James can sleep anywhere!)
I was about to do the same when I realized
we were not alone. Someone else was in
the barn. It was another dog and he was
not pleased to see me.

"Who goes there?" he growled from
the shadows.

I felt my **hackles** prickle, but I
answered **pawlitely**. "I am Stamp, from
Barnaby Station."

The dog came closer. I kept my tail in
a **neutral pawsition**. James and I believe
in good manners.

"Well, Stamp of Barnaby Station," said the dog, "what are you doing in my barn?"

Now that he was closer I saw he was a border collie, like me. I also saw he was quite old. He had tan cheeks and his muzzle and eyebrows were going gray.

"I am a junior dog, traveling with my master. We needed somewhere dry to sleep," I said, still pawlitely.

"Then you may stay. And you had better make the most of it," said the old dog. "It won't be dry by morning. By the way, my name's Rusty." Rusty walked over to the doorway of the barn and sniffed the air. "More rain's coming," he said. "And there's going to be a lot of it. I am worried about the sheep in **Tea Tree Five**."

"Why are you worried?" I asked. I never waste a chance to learn more.

"I am a sheepdog," said Rusty. "My

first duty is to guard and guide my sheep."

"What's your second duty?" I asked.

"My second duty is to guard and guide *other* sheep. My *third* duty is to obey my master's commands."

"Is Glen Pepper a good master?"

"He is a kind master, but he doesn't understand the impawtance of sheep. Not as I do. Now go to sleep."

I did as Rusty suggested.

I woke when someone breathed on my nose. I opened my eyes. Two eyes stared back at me.

"Who are you?" I asked.

"I am Ulysses Sinbad Cook," said the owner of the eyes. "It is raining."

"I know," I said. "What are you doing here?"

"Keeping dry. Go to sleep, dog."

"But I *was* asleep," I pointed out.

The cat—I thought it was a cat—
narrowed its eyes at me. "You are getting
sleeeeepy . . . "

When I woke in the morning, it
was still raining and there were puddles
everywhere. My favorite blanket was
wringing wet.

"Where's the cat?" I asked Rusty.

Rusty stared at me. "What cat?"

"Ulysses Sinbad Cook," I said.

"Ulysses Sinbad Cook?" repeated
Rusty. "You must have been dreaming."

Stamp's Glossary

Wool blanket. Wool blankets are warm and snug. They are pawfect for scratching into a comfy bed.

Hackles. The hair along a dog's back stands up if we feel threatened. It makes us look bigger.

Neutral pawsition. A dog's tail tells a lot about the dog's mood. A neutral tail (low but relaxed) = wary but friendly.

Pawlite. Rude dogs are not popular. I keep telling Ace this, but she doesn't believe me.

Shaking hands. What humans do instead of sniffing bottoms. It is a greeting. James has taught me to shake hands.

Tea Tree Five. Farmers often give their paddocks names or numbers.

A Word on Tails!

You can tell a lot from the position of a dog's tail.

- A tail tucked in between the hind legs means the dog is frightened. Be careful. Frightened dogs sometimes snap.
- A tail carried low and relaxed means the dog is in a neutral mood.
- A tail wagging gently means the dog is happy.
- A tail carried stiffly upright or upright with a waving tip means the dog could be feeling aggressive.

Chapter Three

Rising Water

"Look at that!" said James. We stood in the doorway and looked out. The rain had stopped, but the whole yard was covered in mud and puddles. "Let's see what we can do to help."

I looked around for the cat, but it was not in sight. Maybe I really did dream it.

We splashed over to the house.

"Just as well you're here, James," said Glen Pepper. "There are some campers stranded by the creek. I went down this morning to warn them to move, but the water had already come up around their car so they couldn't drive out."

Mrs. Pepper handed sandwiches to James and Glen, then gave Rusty and me a dog biscuit each. "Here you are, boys . . . " She smiled at James. "These are Rusty's favorites. Tidge-Treats. Glen has them sent from Doggeroo, especially."

I wagged my tail in thanks. I am a forgiving dog.

"I'm taking the boat to ferry them out," said Glen.

We went to the shed where the tractor, trailer, plow and other farm **implements** were kept. There was a small boat slung from the rafters. James and Glen used a **winch** to lower it onto the trailer.

Glen drove the tractor down a track towards the creek. James and I sat on the trailer beside Rusty.

"We should be moving sheep, not bothering with humans," growled Rusty. "Humans can look after themselves."

Glen stopped the tractor on the edge of what used to be a creek. Now it looked like a lake. Out in the water was a camper. The water was halfway up the sides. The car it was hitched to was almost completely underwater.

Two people sat on the roof of the camper. One waved when he saw us.

"Help!" he called. "The water's still rising!"

"And we've lost Pusskins!" wailed the other person.

"This looks bad," said Glen. "When I was here half an hour ago, it was only

halfway up the doors. They could have walked out then, but they didn't want to get wet."

James helped Glen drag the boat off the trailer and into the floodwater. He signaled me to stay where I was.

I sat next to Rusty, who was still grumbling. "Humans should look after themselves," he kept saying. "The *sheep* need us to **pawtect** them."

"Humans have to look after humans too," I said.

"I **suppaws** so," admitted Rusty.

We watched the boat putter across the water. Trees and the tops of fence posts poked through the surface. The boat rocked as James helped the two people down from the camper roof.

"That boat will tip over if they're not careful," said Rusty.

"James won't let that happen," I said.

Rusty sniffed. As a junior dog, I had to respect Rusty. (Pepper Plains Farm was his **territory**, after all.) But he did seem to grumble a lot. He always thought something bad was going to happen.

I decided I would learn what I could from him, but I would not be so **pawsimistic**. As James says, if things go wrong, we can find a way to fix them.

Glen took the campers back to the house to get dry. James, Rusty and I decided to walk back.

"If you're still worried about those sheep, James and I will help you move them somewhere safe," I said.

"Right!" Rusty wagged his tail. "Let's go!"

He set off at a trot and I followed him.

"Stamp!" called James. "That's not the way back to the house!"

I stopped and waved my tail. Then, because James hadn't actually told me to come back, I followed Rusty towards some tea trees.

James jogged after us, splashing and sliding in the wet grass. "Stamp! What—Oh!"

We'd come to a gate. Beyond that, a flock of **ewes** stood in the water.

"Baa! Baaaa! *Baaaaddd!*" they yelled when they saw Rusty.

"Yes, bad. We help now," called Rusty.

Dogs and sheep don't speak the same language, of-paws, but we know how to communicate with sheep and cattle in a few simple words. We have to. How else could we do our jobs?

Stamp's Glossary

Ewe. A female sheep.

Implements. Various large tools used with tractors while working on farms. They include plows, harrows and seed drills.

Pawsimistic. Gloomy, always thinking things will go wrong.

Pawtect. Protect, for dogs.

Suppaws. Suppose, for dogs.

Territory. A home, farm, yard or area that belongs to a dog. (Ace says I have to add that if the territory belongs to a terrier or a terrier mix like her, it's called a **terriertory**.)

Winch. Used to lift, pull or lower a weight too heavy for humans to handle alone.

Chapter Four
Shifting Sheep

Rusty barked an order at James. "Open the gate!"

James looked around. "That water's still rising," he said. "I guess they'd be safer up in a higher paddock."

"Get on with it, boy!" Rusty barked.

James opened the gate and pulled it back. Rusty darted through, leaping through the water to round the sheep into a bunch. "Take the left side," he told me. "Watch out for that small ewe. She's difficult." To the sheep, he barked, "Obey the young dog!"

James picked up a stick and pointed it behind the sheep. It was one of the signals we had practiced. I darted around the sheep in the opposite direction.

Together Rusty and I bunched the sheep and drove them up through the paddock towards higher ground. James sent me a whistle signal to keep following while he ran ahead to open the next gate. He directed us with the pointing stick and the sheep dripped and baaaed and fussed up through the gate.

"Good boy, Stamp," said James when he had closed the gate. I wagged my tail.

As a border collie, I was bred to work with sheep and cattle, so herding them comes naturally to me. James and I have

been working as a team ever since I was very young. We love it. Doing things you do well is one of the best things in life.

"Good dog, Rusty," James added, giving him a quick pat.

Rusty sniffed the air. "More rain coming," he said to me. Then he turned to the sheep. "All well now," he told them. He waved his tail. I saw he was happy with the job we'd done. So was I.

Glen was really happy we had moved the sheep.

"I should have done it earlier," he said. "I got distracted by the campers."

"He's always distracted by something," growled Rusty. "You can never trust humans to do anything impawtant."

"I trust James," I said.

"Your human seems to have more sense than most," agreed Rusty. "Glen never gets down to impawtant things. He should have found me an **apprentice** by now. I'm not getting any younger." He looked at me. "You want a job? You and I work well together."

"I have a job," I said. "I am James's companion. I hope you get an apprentice soon. A young dog could learn a lot from you, Rusty. You are fair and you give clear directions."

"Your dog seemed to know the right paddock to put the sheep in," James said to Glen.

Glen nodded. "He's a good old boy. My brother trained him up ten years ago. When he retired from farming, Rusty came to us. My brother reckoned Rusty would never be happy without sheep. I see his point. He's a working dog, through and through." He laughed. "Sometimes I reckon he knows more about this job than I do. Oh well . . . " He looked at the sky. "We'll take some hay out while the rain holds off. There's not a lot of grass in that hill paddock." He sighed. "I guess the grass in Tea Tree Five and the Creek Paddock will die off if the flood stays up. Just too much water."

Glen was as pawsimistic as Rusty!

Rusty and I rode on the trailer with

James to feed hay to the sheep.

"Baaaa! Hay damp!" protested a small ewe. She was the one Rusty had said was difficult.

"Hay will get damper if you don't eat quickly," said Rusty.

The ewe goggled at him and started chewing as fast as she could.

Rusty waved his tail.

After that we fed hay to the cows.

"Wet hay. I protest!" complained a leggy heifer.

"It will be wetter if you don't hurry and eat it," said Rusty.

The heifer snorted, but picked up a big mouthful of hay.

By then it was dinnertime. Mrs. Pepper had driven the campers into town, so it was just the Peppers and James at the table.

James washed and dried my muddy paws and legs and told me to sit quietly behind the couch. I did as I was told. I didn't want Mrs. Pepper to send me back to the barn. The smell of wet hay would make me sneeze. I ate my kibble and settled down to lick my paws.

James had given me a good toweling, but I still felt damp. I really wanted to have a good roll and scrub around on the carpet, but I knew Mrs. Pepper wouldn't like that.

The phone rang and Glen got up and answered it.

"It's Tory Maxwell," said Glen, putting his hand over the receiver. "Tory and Dave are our neighbors downriver," he told James. "Dave's had a fall and Tory has taken him to the doctor." I peeped out from behind the couch and saw Glen pause to shake his head. "The problem is, he was on his way to shift his sheep from the island, and now he needs help . . ."

Mrs. Pepper sighed. "Maybe you and James could do it," she said.

Glen spoke into the phone. "Don't worry, Tory. We'll see to it. We hope Dave's okay . . . No, of course it's no trouble."

He hung up. "He'll be fine, Tory
says." He turned to James. "James . . . ?"

"Sure," said James. "Stamp and I will
be happy to help move the sheep."

Stamp's Glossary

Apprentice. A younger dog or person learning
the job from someone more experienced.
Heifer. A young cow which has had no more
than one calf.

Chapter Five

The Causeway

James jumped up. "I'll get my jacket." He whistled to me. "Come on, Stamp." He turned to Glen. "Will we need the boat?"

"No, the island has a **causeway**."

"A causeway?" said James. "How does that work?"

"Years ago, Dave's dad got a bulldozer and pushed up a pile of rocks and soil to make a kind of solid bridge so he could drive across from the riverbank to the island," explained Glen. "Tory says we'll just need to open a gate at the island end to let the sheep out."

We all piled into the Fourby. Rusty and I sat in the backseat. As James started the engine, the first heavy drops of rain hit the roof and windshield.

"I told you it wasn't over yet," said Rusty.

The windshield and windows fogged up and I felt my fur getting damp again. Water was spreading everywhere from the creek and the rain and the river.

"Down this track," said Glen. James turned the Fourby down the track after engaging **four-wheel drive**. We bounced and jolted over stones, with water spread out on either side. The roaring sound I'd heard the day before was much louder now. The Fourby's engine roared too. It lurched as we rumbled up onto a stony ridge of the causeway.

"Not far now," said Rusty. "But I think we might be too late."

I thought he was being pawsimistic again, but it turned out he was right. James slowed down suddenly and I heard him say, "Uh-oh," over the noise.

I got up and put my paws against the window ledge, but it was raining too hard to see out.

"We'd better check how deep it is," said James in a loud voice.

He and Glen got out of the Fourby. James left the door open, so of-paws Rusty and I jumped between the front seats and out onto the causeway.

I had never seen anything like it before. The Fourby's headlights shone through the rain and lit up the rough

surface of the causeway. After that we
saw just a few broken chunks of rock and
a wild surge of water at the edge of the
swollen river.

"The flood's washed out a chunk of the causeway!" yelled Glen.

"Can we make it across?" James yelled back.

"No. We'd better back up. More of it could break away any minute."

"What about the sheep?" James pointed to the bunch of just-visible sheep huddled behind the gate on the island at the far end of the causeway.

Glen shook his head. "Can't get to them. It's far too dangerous. They should be okay if the water doesn't rise any— holey dooley! Look at that!"

We all jumped back as a surge of water came *up*stream.

"That's the tide coming in!" yelled Glen as waves lapped against the bank. "We're not far from the mouth of the river."

James jumped into the Fourby and backed it away from the broken bit of causeway while Rusty and I waited with Glen.

"Those sheep are in trouble!" said Rusty. The sheep, who were baa-baa-*baaaddding*, seemed to agree.

And that's when James asked if we should get the boat, instead. But Glen pointed out a tree sailing past in the water. It was a huge tree. I saw the roots, still caught up in clay and lumps of rock, sticking up above the water. You would not want to collide with that!

What could we do?

Rusty tried to get Glen's attention, but it was hard over all the commotion.

I was about to make a suggestion.

I'm sure you remember what happened next . . .

One minute Rusty stood beside me, with his ears and eyebrows streaming with water. The next . . . he leapt out into the river and disappeared.

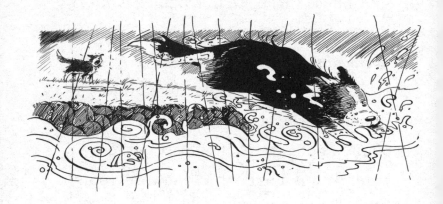

Stamp's Glossary

Causeway. A raised road or ridge of ground connecting an island to the mainland.

Four-wheel drive. Sending engine power to all four wheels of a vehicle instead of just to two. We dogs have four-paw drive.

Chapter Six
Good-bye, Rusty

"Rusty! Rusty!" I barked as loudly as I
could. I rushed to the edge of the water
and ran up and down. I thought I saw
something bobbing on the water near the
floating tree and then the tree rolled in
the current. The roots whooshed through
the water and the tree swept on.

"Rusty!" I leapt towards the water, but
James grabbed me.

"No, Stamp!"

"Rusty!" yelled Glen. "Come back here! Rusty!"

I tried to struggle free. Water was running in my ears and eyes. I had to save Rusty!

"No, Stamp." James set me down on the ground and knelt beside me, holding my collar with one hand and stroking my wet head with the other. "It's just too dangerous."

"Rusty!" I barked. If it was too dangerous for me, it was too dangerous for Rusty. "Rusty!" I barked again.

But no one barked back.

"Rusty . . ." said Glen, but he wasn't calling out anymore.

The sheep went on baaaing. The rain went on pouring. The river kept on roaring. Another piece of causeway crumbled into the flood.

James got up, but he kept a firm hold on my collar. I looked up at him to see how he was going to rescue Rusty. Maybe he had a rope?

It took a while for me to understand that James wasn't going to rescue Rusty. No one was. And that wasn't because Glen and James didn't want to rescue him. It was because there was no way to do it.

Floods are dangerous things.

I think that was the first time I realized there were some things James and I couldn't fix.

"We'd better get out of here," said Glen, as more chunks crumbled off the causeway.

James looked downstream. Glen stared in the same direction. "The poor old fellow. I wish I'd grabbed hold of him," he murmured.

"You couldn't have known he'd jump in," said James.

"I should have known." Glen looked sadly at the river. "Rusty lived for sheep. He *loved* sheep. I should have grabbed him . . . We'll be in trouble ourselves if the rest of this causeway goes."

"What about the neighbor's sheep?"

Glen shrugged. "There's nothing we can do about them tonight. I'll give Tory a call in the morning. She'll understand. There's no way she would want us in any danger."

That reminded me of what I'd said to Rusty. Humans have to take care of humans. Farmers live with **livestock**. They like them and care for them well. But things go wrong sometimes, and farmers like Glen and Dad Barnaby have to be practical about it. They do the best they can.

Silently, we all got into the Fourby. There was no room to turn around, so James backed it up slowly. When he looked over his shoulder to see where to drive, I saw that his face looked sad.

I was sad myself. I sat alone in the backseat and I could still smell Rusty's scent and see the prints of his paws on the window ledge.

Stamp's Glossary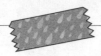

Livestock. Cattle, sheep and pigs and other farm animals.

Chapter Seven

Wet Hay

It kept right on raining all night, but the next morning, the sun came out. The whole of Pepper Plains Farm was like a muddy sea with islands of land here and there.

That night James and I had slept on a blow-up mattress in the family room. Mrs. Pepper pretended she didn't know I was there. I didn't sleep as well as

usual—I missed my favorite blanket. I generally give it a good scruff around with my nose and paws before I settle to sleep.

"There's flooding all along the river as far up as Cowfork and Doggeroo," said Glen at breakfast. He'd been listening to the radio. "It's worse here, though because we're so close to the river."

"My garden is going to be a mess," said Mrs. Pepper. "Half my lettuces and beets will be floating out to sea by now!"

"Everything is a mess," said Glen. "We won't know how bad it is until the water level drops. At least the livestock are all right so far." He sighed and looked at the floor. "I'm really going to miss old Rusty. I can't believe he's gone. Remember how he always knew when we got his Tidge-Treat biscuits in the mail?"

"I'll help out with the cleanup," said

James quickly. I could tell he didn't want to talk about Rusty. But I didn't want to believe he was gone, either.

I went out to the porch and sniffed the air. Was there going to be more rain? It didn't smell like it.

If Rusty was here, he'd be saying, "It isn't over yet." I wished Rusty *was* here. He was pawsimistic, but he always did his duty.

Some ducks swam by in what was probably Mrs. Pepper's rose garden. Maybe I could herd all of them together, just for something to do. I barked for attention and gave them **the eye.**

"Don't even think of it, dog," quacked the lead duck. "Us ducks are taking over the world."

"Waark waark waark!" They all quacked with laughter and waggled their tails.

At least someone was happy.

James and Glen went out in the boat to check on the cows and sheep. "You stay here, Stamp," said James.

The water dropped all through the

day. By dinnertime, the garden was clear. Of-paws it was covered in mud, wet hay and lots of sticks. The barn was standing clear of the water too. I wondered what had happened to my favorite blanket.

We slept in the family room again.

The next morning, the water had dropped back even farther. There were still pools in low-lying parts of the paddocks, but the fast-flowing water had gone back into the river and the creeks, where it belonged. The noise from the Jeandabah River had softened.

James and Glen went out to mend some of the broken fences. I got tired of sitting on the porch where James had left me. I trotted down to the barn to find my favorite blanket.

I poked around in the wet hay and found one of James's blankets washed up hard against one of the walls. It was tangled up in **baling twine.**

I sniffed around. Yes! I caught a whiff of my own blanket. Then I caught another familiar scent. I went to investigate. It was another blanket, wet and crumpled but quite thick. It smelled of Rusty.

I was glad Glen had given Rusty a cozy blanket. Some **working dogs** don't have their own blankets. Dad Barnaby always says a good dog deserves good food, a good bed and good attention.

I shook off my sad thoughts and went back to my own blanket. If I dragged it out into the yard it might dry enough for me to scruff it into a comfortable spot to sit until James came back.

I sighed, and sneezed. Then I sneezed again and again. The air in the barn was thick and damp and too warm.

I left the blanket where it was and went back to the porch to wait for James.

When he got back, he was blotched with mud. His boots were caked with it.

"Oh, hi, Stamp!" he said. I'd jumped up and trotted to meet him. He bent to pat me, and I grabbed his sleeve and tugged.

That's a game we played when I was a puppy. James would hide something and I would tug his sleeve until he came with me to look for it.

He let me lead him along to the barn.

I sniffed and sneezed. James sneezed too. "This isn't good," said James.

James ran back to the house to fetch Glen. I pulled my blanket out into the muddy yard.

Stamp's Glossary

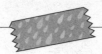

Baling twine. A strong string used to hold hay bales together.

The eye. Border collies use their strong eye gaze to communicate with sheep.

Working dogs. Some dogs are bred to be pets. Others are bred to work. Border collies are working dogs although they can be pets as well.

Chapter Eight
Bank Patrol

James and the Peppers started unstacking hay and restacking the dry bales to the side.

"I want to save as much of the hay as I can. The wettest stuff will go moldy," said Glen. "But Wendy will use it as mulch on her garden, so it won't be wasted."

While they were busy, three pickups drove into the yard. "You guys want some help?" yelled one of the drivers.

"Yes, please!" said James. "We're saving as much hay as we can."

"Okay!"

In no time, six more pairs of boots were tramping in and out of the barn. I noticed two of the **volunteers** were the campers we'd rescued from the flood.

"About time, too," said a voice behind my left ear.

I jumped. "Who-who?"

"Hoo-hoo? Are you an owl or a dog?" A smoke-colored cat strolled around and sat down to stare at me. I stared back.

"Ulysses Sinbad Cook?" I said. "Where have you been?"

"Around," said the cat. It kept on staring. "Where's the other dog?"

I sighed. It still hurt to think of Rusty. "He tried to save some sheep and got washed away down the river," I said sadly.

"And he's not back yet?" said the cat.

"He was washed away!" I snapped.

Ulysses Sinbad Cook blinked. "Dogs can swim."

"Of-paws we can swim," I said, "but—"

We were interrupted by a glad cry of

"*There* you are, Pusskins!" as the female camper rushed towards us.

"Pusskins?" I said.

The cat tilted his head. "It's time for my big reunion scene," he said. "And do not call me 'Pusskins.' My name is Ulysses Sinbad Cook and don't you forget it." He got up and swaggered over to his owner. "By the way," he called out as she scooped him up in her arms, "I hope you find your pal. You shouldn't give up on him."

I watched Ulysses smooching his owner.

Then I decided to go down to the river for a **bank patrol**, just in case. James hadn't actually told me to stay where I was. I walked a little way and looked over my shoulder. James didn't call me back.

I trotted down through the paddocks

towards the river. The grass was muddy and it smelled likc a swamp. The river was still roaring away, but it was back inside its banks.

The sheep were back in Tea Tree Five, picking at the grass.

"Baaaaa, young dog . . ." one of them said. "What wrong?"

"Where *our* dog?" asked another.

"All well," I barked. I couldn't tell them their dog, Rusty, had been swept away.

I picked my way along the edge of the bank and nosed among the **debris**. I found all sorts of things . . . old rags, carrots, odd shoes and even a broken bucket.

The sun shone down and I felt it drawing the water up from the ground. The puddles I wandered through were warm now.

I sniff-sniffed the ground. Rabbits and birds had been there today. It was good to know they had found somewhere safe during the flood.

I crawled under fences. The wires were hung with a web of grass and twigs. There was hay caught up in hedges, and bits of twine tangled in fallen branches.

The wind blew up the river, ruffling the water. I sniffed and smelled salt. That wind must have come up from the beach. I sniffed again, smelling salt, fish, mud and more mud. I smelled wet sheep.

I trotted on until I saw broken ground ahead. It all looked different in daylight, but I realized I had almost reached the causeway.

I climbed the slope and picked my way along the rough track. There were the heavy wheel marks the Fourby had left. I smelled a whiff of James and Glen and there was a faint scent of my own paws . . . and of poor old Rusty.

The muddy ground was very slippery. When I had gone as far as it was safe, I looked out over the river to the island.

It looked much bigger today. I barked, "Sheep! Sheep! Report!"

Nothing happened, so I barked again. "Sheep! Sheep!"

"Baaaaa!" Seven ewes came out of the scrub. "Baaaadddd!" they wailed.

They looked muddy. Their legs were brown and there was mud all over their bellies. But they were all right.

"All there?" I barked.

"Baaaaaadddd!" they yelled. Then the oldest ewe answered properly. "All here."

Old Rusty would have been pleased about that, I thought.

"All well!" I barked to the sheep. "Stay safe!"

I sniffed the air again. Sheep. Mud. Salt. Rotting carrots. Rusty. Fish . . .

Rusty? How could I be smelling Rusty on the wind here? This was not where we had stood. This ground had been underwater when we were here before.

I sniffed upstream. I sniffed downstream. I peered down the river. In the distance, I saw a fallen tree lying half in and half out of the water. Could it

be the one we saw carried along on the flood? I remembered thinking it would be a bad thing to collide with in the river. You could get caught in the branches.

Could—

I seemed to hear Ulysses Sinbad Cook's voice in my ear. *"I hope you find your pal. You shouldn't give up on him."*

Of-paws! Rusty was a wise dog. He was an experienced dog. He had lived by the river for years. And what else had Ulysses said? *"Dogs can swim."*

I ran along the edge of the water, hopping over piles of debris, keeping a lookout for snakes. I stopped and sniffed again. Mud, fish, salt, rotting carrots . . . Rusty!

"Report! Report! Report!" I barked. "Rusty! Report!"

I came up to the broken tree. Yes, there were the roots sticking up, though most of the clay had washed out now. The branches were full of junk from the flood. Twine tangled around the twigs, and bits of torn plastic fluttered in the wind.

I sniffed hard. I could definitely smell Rusty somewhere! He was here!

"Report!" I barked.

"Hello, Stamp," growled a weak voice. "It took you long enough to find me."

Stamp's Glossary

Bank patrol. Exploring along a bank to see what I could see.

Debris. Trash and other things left behind after a flood or a storm.

Volunteers. People who help out without payment.

Chapter Nine

Twine

Poor Rusty was caught in the broken tree. Some of the baling twine was hooked in his collar and tangled on a branch. He looked terrible. The mud was all churned up where he had struggled.

"Are the sheep all right on the island?" he asked.

"Yes! I just saw them, but the impawtant thing is—"

"Are my sheep safe?"

"They're fine. They miss you. But Rusty, you need help."

"Help me then," said Rusty. "Can you bite through this twine for me? I can't reach it."

I clambered through the branches until I got close to Rusty's neck. It looked

sore. He had rubbed it trying to break free.

The twine was twisted and knotted, but I got my teeth around one of the knots. It tasted terrible, but I pretended it was a **rawhide chew**.

I chewed and pulled, but I couldn't break through. "I'll get James," I said, and dashed off.

I was nearly back to the barn when I heard James whistling our *Where are you?* signal.

"Here! Here!" I barked. "Here!"

"Stamp!" James ran across the paddock. "*There* you are, Stamp! Stamp, where have you been?"

I barked again. "Here! Here!" Then I turned and dashed back to Rusty. I knew James would follow.

When James caught up he didn't waste

any time. "Rusty!" he said. He took out his pocket knife and carefully cut through the twine.

Gently, he picked Rusty up and carried him back to the barn.

Glen, Mrs. Pepper, the campers and the volunteers were all sitting on the dry hay bales drinking mugs of tea. Ulysses Sinbad Cook was draped over his owner's shoulders like a shawl.

Glen looked up when he heard us coming. He jumped up and came to meet us. "Rusty! Is he—"

"He's a bit knocked around, but I think he'll be all right," said James, grinning.

"But where did you find him?" Glen took Rusty from James. The old dog wagged his tail. Glen hugged him close to his chest.

"He was caught up in a fallen tree. He must have washed up on the bank. Stamp found him. I just helped untangle him."

Glen set Rusty down and took off his collar. He looked up at Mrs. Pepper. "Wendy, can you . . . ?"

"I'll get the first aid box," said Mrs. Pepper. "Bring the poor old chap into the house, Glen. I'll make him up a bed in the laundry room. Then we'll call the vet."

"Don't need a vet," protested Rusty, but his tail was still wagging.

Glen looked happier than I had ever seen him. "This calls for Tidge-Treats for two!" he cried.

Stamp's Glossary

Rawhide chew. Rawhide strips or knots made especially for dogs to chew.

Chapter Ten
Meet Ace

By the time we left Pepper Plains Farm,
everything had almost dried out and
Rusty was back to his old self again.

"Rusty gets along really well with your
Stamp," said Glen. "I don't suppose you'd
like to stay on?"

"No, thanks," said James. "We'll be
on our way. We're going to see Cousin
Jeannie, the vet at Cowfork. Maybe she'll
know of a pup you could train up."

"Rusty would like that, I think," said Mrs. Pepper. She looked down at Rusty, who was gnawing a meaty bone. "What do you reckon, old boy?"

Rusty left one paw on the bone and wagged his tail. "Finally!" he said to me. "I'll get an apprentice! Glen will have to put in a permanent double order for Tidge-Treats!"

I was surprised. Rusty just made a *joke*!

And so it was settled. James and I said good-bye to Pepper Plains and drove away. The last thing I saw was Rusty's blanket flapping in the wind from the porch railing. Mrs. Pepper had washed it and it had come up like new.

It was good to be on the road again.

The Fourby had dried out and I sat up in my **harness** and stuck my nose out the window. At first, the smell of the flood hung on the wind, but as we got farther and farther from Pepper Plains, the normal smells of grass and trees, birds and sunshine took over. It was dark by the time we reached Cowfork. We camped at a place called Jeandabah Park.

In the morning, James packed everything back in the Fourby and then spread out our map. "I know Cousin Jeannie lives somewhere around here . . ." he muttered. "Ah . . . here it is. Cowfork

House and Pet Vet Clinic. Maybe she'll give us some breakfast."

We arrived at Jeannie's place at seven o'clock. "I hope she's up," said James. He tapped on the door.

After a bit, it opened and two heads popped out. One was a woman with a ponytail. The other, which was much lower down, was a Jack Russell terrier.

"Yes?" they said together. The woman added, "That's a fine dog, but if you've come for the clinic, we're not open yet."

James smiled. "Hi, Jeannie . . . I'm your cousin, James Barnaby, and this is Stamp."

"Oh! I didn't recognize you. You were having your tenth birthday when I saw you last. I remember you said you wanted to be a vet."

"I'm considering it. That's partly why

I called in to talk to you. We were also
hoping you might know of a young collie
or kelpie that would suit a farmer down at
Pepper Plains."

James and Jeannie went off, chatting away. That left me face-to-face with the Jack Russell. Terriers can be snappy sometimes, but this one seemed friendly. "I'm Trump," she said. "Welcome to Pet Vet Clinic. I'm Dr. Jeannie's Animal Liaison Officer. If you're looking for pups, you'd better come this way."

We followed our humans out into a sunny yard where three dogs were waiting in runs. A kelpie pup and a half-grown spaniel were having a game with a ball. The third dog was a rather rough-haired little thing. She turned her sharp little nose in my direction and peered at me through her fringe.

"What are you looking at?" she snapped.

"Stay away from that one," said Trump. "She's trouble."

"The spaniel is boarding here for a week," said Jeannie, "but the kelpie is available for adoption. He's a nice young fellow, but not a pedigreed dog like your handsome Stamp."

"He might be just the dog for the Peppers," said James. "Their old collie is getting on in years, but he and Stamp got quite friendly. Here's their number if you'd like to give them a call."

Jeannie took the piece of paper. "I'll

do that. I'd like to get the pup settled with a steady older dog. Would they look after him well do you think?"

"It's a working farm, but they give their old dog Tidge-Treats," said James with a grin. "Stamp seemed to enjoy them."

Jeannie laughed. "Trump loves Tidge-Treats too. Now, have you folks had breakfast?"

James grinned. "Not yet."

"Okay! Scrambled eggs it is." Jeannie turned to lead the way into the house.

"Who's this one?" said James, pointing to the third dog.

She looked at him and lifted her lip.

"Oh that . . ." Jeannie frowned. "I have no idea what we're going to do with her."

"Oh?" James clicked his tongue to the little dog. She lifted the other side of her lip. "What is she?"

"Some kind of terrier I think. There could be some foxie in there . . . maybe a bit of Jack Russell. Some corgi, maybe. Or a bit of doxie. Even a drop of poodle." She shrugged. "She was purchased for a birthday present and then the owners lost interest. She was cute as a pup, apparently, but she wasn't housebroken and she chased their cat. Then she tore up someone's clothes and ate half a teddy bear."

James laughed. "That sounds like a typical pup."

"Yes . . . and now she's here with me." She sniffed.

James crouched by the fence and held out his fingers.

"I wouldn't do that," said Jeannie. "She—"

"Ouch!" James pulled his hand back.

"—bites," Jeannie finished.

"What did you do that for?" I asked the little dog.

"He looked mean."

"No, he isn't. He—"

She snarled.

Jeannie sighed. "As far as I can tell she's in good shape, but I have no idea who could take her on. She doesn't like other dogs or cats, cockatoos or people . . . "

"What *does* she like?" asked James.

"Food," said Jeannie. She took some Tidge-Treats out of her pocket and gave one each to the kelpie and the spaniel. "Good boys, gently now. Here you are, Trump and Stamp . . . would you like a treat?"

I took mine pawlitely. It tasted just as good as the ones Rusty had.

Suddenly, the little dog jumped at the fence and yapped wildly. "Treat! Treat! Treat!"

"May I?" said James.

Jeannie handed him a treat. "Just mind your fingers!"

The little dog hurled herself at the fence and snapped.

"Sit," said James.

"She doesn't sit," said Jeannie.

James grinned. "She's naughty, isn't she?" He tossed the Tidge-Treat in the air.

The little dog caught it.

"Clever, too."

"Oh, she's clever enough," said Jeannie. "She just needs someone who has time and patience and a lot of experience and maybe a well-trained dog to act as an example for her."

"Okay," said James. "Stamp gets along well with other dogs and we're always up for a challenge. We'll take her!"

Jeannie stared at him. "Really?"

"Don't take her," Trump said to me. "She's wild and weird and impawsible!"

The little dog glared at me and lifted her lip . . .

And that's how we came to drive away two days later with our new companion. James said he was sure we'd soon teach her some manners . . .

He named her Ace.

Stamp's Glossary

Harness. What I wear to keep me safe in a vehicle. A doggie seat belt.

A Word on Approaching Strange Dogs

When approaching a dog you don't know, it is better to ask the owner before you go near.

Always offer the back of your hand slowly and gently. If the dog stiffens, cringes or looks uncomfortable, back away.

Don't stare straight at the dog. Some dogs find this frightening or challenging.